MW00571215

Answers

1. **d.** Did you guess that Winona Ryder would pick an album by her ex's band?
2. **e.** Tara Lipinski is *thrilled* by Michael Jackson.
3. **a.** Could Alice Cooper like those new Gap commercials more than we suspect?
4. **c.** It seems Shaq can't live without the Queen of rock.
5. **b.** Fabio welcomes Journey with "Open Arms."

Here are a few more celebrity music secrets you'll find in this indispensable guide:

*Which long-running band appears—twice—on Guns N' Roses musician Slash's hit list?
*What legendary musician puts Little Richard at the top of his list?
*What Top-40 heartthrob considers Willie Nelson a favorite?
. . . and much, much more

MICHAEL FRIEDMAN is a former music business executive and artist manager who has landed record deals for many prominent artists. Under his own record label, Vibra Cobra Records (www.vibracobra.com), he has launched the careers of several rocks bands. He lives in Los Angeles.

STAR★TUNES

Celebrities Reveal the Top Ten Albums They Can't Live Without

Edited by Michael Friedman

A PLUME BOOK

PLUME
Published by the Penguin Group
Penguin Putnam Inc., 375 Hudson Street, New York, New York 10014, U.S.A.
Penguin Books Ltd, 27 Wrights Lane, London W8 5TZ, England
Penguin Books Australia Ltd, Ringwood, Victoria, Australia
Penguin Books Canada Ltd, 10 Alcorn Avenue, Toronto, Ontario, Canada M4V 3B2
Penguin Books (N.Z.) Ltd, 182–190 Wairau Road, Auckland 10, New Zealand

Penguin Books Ltd, Registered Offices:
Harmondsworth, Middlesex, England

First published by Plume,
a member of Penguin Putnam Inc.

First Printing, May 2001
1   3   5   7   9   10   8   6   4   2

Ⓟ REGISTERED TRADEMARK—MARCA REGISTRADA

LIBRARY OF CONGRESS CATALOGING-IN-PUBLICATION DATA

Star tunes: celebrities reveal the top ten albums they can't live without /
edited by Michael Friedman.
p.   cm.
Includes index.
ISBN 0-452-28234-9
1. Popular music—Discography.   2. Celebrities—Discography.
I. Friedman, Michael.
ML156.4.P6 S84 2001
016.78164'0266—dc21   00-053730

Printed in the United States of America
Set in Trade Gothic

BOOKS ARE AVAILABLE AT QUANTITY DISCOUNTS WHEN USED TO PROMOTE PRODUCTS OR SERVICES.
FOR INFORMATION PLEASE WRITE TO PREMIUM MARKETING DIVISION, PENGUIN PUTNAM INC.,
375 HUDSON STREET, NEW YORK, NEW YORK 10014.

Contents

Introduction

We've all heard the sayings before—*Life happens while you're listening to music; Without music life would be a mistake; You are what you listen to.* Albums or CDs, depending on the era in which you were born, cause us to have emotional reactions. A great record can fill us with energy or reduce us to tears. Sometimes both at once. Records let us dream, they let us feel, and they let us remember. They enhance our lives.

I wanted to find out about some of the music that inspired, influenced, and moved the celebrities I admired, so I set about putting together *Star Tunes*. I got in touch with actors, actresses, singers, bands, musicians, comedians, directors, writers, professional athletes, and many other kinds of stars, and they sent me their lists. Some of the lists had me running for the record store, and I got a real musical education. This made me think about what would be on my own list, and I decided it would look something like this:

> Kiss – *Alive!*
>
> Dinosaur Jr. – *You're Living All Over Me*
>
> Rush – *A Farewell to Kings*
>
> Hüsker Dü – *New Day Rising*
>
> Devo – *Duty for the Future*
>
> Led Zeppelin – *Houses of the Holy*
>
> David Bowie – *Low*
>
> Kyuss – *Blues for the Red Sun*
>
> Failure – *Fantastic Planet*
>
> Nine Inch Nails – *Pretty Hate Machine*

I had a lot of fun putting *Star Tunes* together, and I hope that—whether you're using it as a music reference guide or simply to gain more insight into the life of your favorite star—you'll have as much fun as I did exploring the music that has touched the lives of these celebrities.

Los Angeles, 2000
vibracobra@mediaone.net

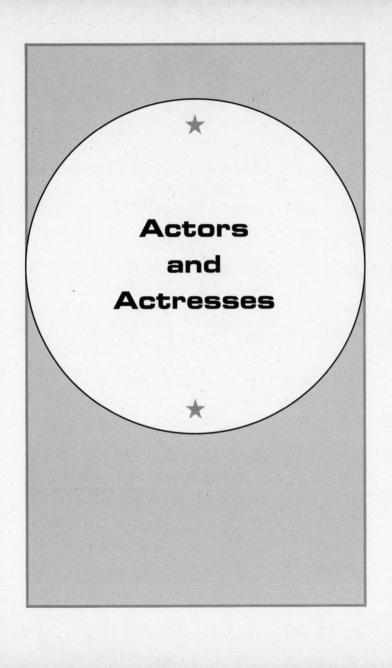

Actors
and
Actresses

HENRY THOMAS
Actor

Van Morrison – *Astral Weeks*

Tom Waits – *Closing Time*

The Beatles – *Revolver*

Miles Davis – *Kind of Blue*

Devo – *Freedom of Choice*

Lucinda Williams – *Sweet Old World*

Stan Getz and João Gilberto – *Getz–Gilberto*

Belle & Sebastian – *If You're Feeling Sinister*

The Pogues – *If I Should Fall from Grace with God*

Willie Nelson – *Greatest Hits (& Some That Will Be)*

PAUL REUBENS
(aka Pee Wee Herman)
Actor

The Jimi Hendrix Experience –
Axis: Bold as Love

The Beatles – *Meet the Beatles!*

Leon Russell – *Leon Russell*

Neneh Cherry – *Raw Like Sushi*

Prince and the Revolution – *Purple Rain*

Nina Rota – *$8^1/_2$ soundtrack*

X – *Los Angeles*

Aretha Franklin – *Aretha's Gold*

The Rolling Stones – *Let It Bleed*

Stevie Wonder – *The Secret Life of Plants*

KIRSTEN DUNST
Actress

Joni Mitchell – *Blue*

Cowboy Junkies – *The Trinity Session*

Les Misérables – Original Broadway
cast recording

Bob Dylan – *Bringing It All Back Home*

Donovan – *Greatest Hits*

Abba – *Gold*

Ben Harper and the Innocent Criminals –
Burn to Shine

Frank Sinatra – *Sinatra Reprise:
The Very Good Years*

Bebel Gilberto – *Tanto Tempo*

Jeff Buckley – *Grace*

Larsen & Talbert

KIRSTEN DUNST

COURTENEY COX ARQUETTE
Actress

Al Green – *Al Green's Greatest Hits*

Bill Withers – *Greatest Hits*

Stevie Wonder – *Songs in the Key of Life*

Van Morrison – *Moondance*

The Beatles – *Rubber Soul*

Earth, Wind and Fire – *The Best of Earth, Wind and Fire, Vol. 1*

Otis Redding – *The Very Best of Otis Redding*

Marvin Gaye – *Anthology*

The Rolling Stones – *Beggars Banquet*

Radiohead – *OK Computer*

SUSAN ANTON
Actress

Stevie Wonder – *Songs in the Key of Life*

Frank Sinatra – *Sinatra at the Sands*

Elton John – *Goodbye Yellow Brick Road*

The Beatles – *Sgt. Pepper's Lonely Hearts Club Band*

The Beatles – *Help!*

Barbra Streisand – *A Happening in Central Park*

Bing Crosby – *White Christmas*

The Beach Boys – *Pet Sounds*

The Doors – *The Doors*

U2 – *The Joshua Tree*

Ali Smith

SANDRA BERNHARD

SANDRA BERNHARD
Actress, comedienne

Carole King – *Tapestry*

Laura Nyro – *Eli and the 13th Confession*

Joni Mitchell – *Court & Spark*

Rolling Stones – *Beggars Banquet*

The Jimi Hendrix Experience –
Are You Experienced?

Marianne Faithfull – *Strange Weather*

Dusty Springfield – *Dusty in Memphis*

Marvin Gaye – *What's Going On*

Fleetwood Mac – *The Dance*

The Pretenders – *Pretenders*

ROSANNA ARQUETTE
Actress

The Beatles – *Revolver*

Genesis – *The Lamb Lies Down on Broadway*

Traffic – *The Low Spark of High Heeled Boys*

Joni Mitchell – *Blue*

Joni Mitchell – *For the Roses*

Led Zeppelin – *(IV)*

Jane's Addiction – *Nothing's Shocking*

Bob Dylan – "Tangled Up in Blue" on
Blood on the Tracks

Kate Bush – *The Kick Inside*

Neil Young – *After the Goldrush*

ALAN THICKE
Actor

Gordon Lightfoot – *Sundown*

Bruce Springsteen – *Born to Run*

Elton John – *Goodbye Yellow Brick Road*

Billy Joel – *Piano Man*

Barry Manilow – *Tryin' to Get the Feeling*

Sting – *The Dream of the Blue Turtles*

Shania Twain – *Come on Over*

Fleetwood Mac – *Rumours*

Eagles – *Hotel California*

DENNIS HOPPER
Actor, director

Ike & Tina Turner – *River Deep Mountain High*

Miles Davis – *Kind of Blue*

Waylon Jennings – *Honky Tonk Heroes*

The Beatles – *Sgt. Pepper's Lonely Hearts Club Band*

Stravinsky – *L'Histoire du Soldat*

Prokofiev – *The Love for Three Oranges*

Bob Dylan – *Pat Garrett & Billy the Kid* original soundtrack

Easy Rider soundtrack

Colors soundtrack

Miles Davis – *Hotspot*

DENNIS HOPPER

CHLOË SEVIGNY
Actress

The Smiths – *The Smiths*

The Smiths – *Meat Is Murder*

The Smiths – *Hatful of Hollow*

The Smiths – *Louder Than Bombs*

The Smiths – *Rank*

The Smiths – *The Queen Is Dead*

Morrissey – *Bona Drag*

Morrissey – *Viva Hate*

Dirty Three – *Ocean Song*

Nico – *The Marble Index*

BILLY BOB THORNTON
Actor, director

The Allman Brothers Band – *Live at Fillmore East*

Pink Floyd – *Dark Side of the Moon*

Frank Zappa – *Hot Rats*

Creedence Clearwater Revival – *Cosmos Factory*

Frank Zappa and the Mothers of Invention –
Burnt Weeny Sandwich

Captain Beefheart and His Magic Band –
Trout Mask Replica

Traffic – *Smiling Phases*

The Beatles – *Abbey Road*

George Jones – *The George Jones Collection*

Jim Reeves – *Welcome to My World:
The Essential Jim Reeves*

Chet Atkins – *The Essential Chet Atkins*

JOSHUA MORROW
Actor, musician

Guns N' Roses – *Appetite for Destruction*

Bon Jovi – *Slippery When Wet*

Dr. Dre – *The Chronic*

Michael Jackson – *Thriller*

The Beastie Boys – *Licensed to Ill*

Nirvana – *Nevermind*

Tom Petty – *Full Moon Fever*

Def Leppard – *Hysteria*

AC/DC – *Back in Black*

Pearl Jam – *Ten*

JOSHUA MORROW

DAVE FOLEY
Actor, comedian

David Bowie – *Lodger*

Elvis Costello and the Attractions –
This Year's Model

The Replacements – *Tim*

The Clash – *London Calling*

XTC – *Black Sea*

Frank Zappa and the Mothers of Invention –
Mothers of Invention

The Beatles – *Revolver*

Liz Phair – *Exile in Guyville*

Billy Bragg – *Workers Playtime*

Rahsaan Roland Kirk – *Volunteered Slavery*

DAVID SCHWIMMER
Actor

Jackson 5 – *ABC*

David Bowie – *Changesbowie*

Duran Duran – *Rio*

The Police – *Synchronicity*

Van Morrison – *Tupelo Honey*

Eagles – *Hotel California*

Prince and the Revolution – *Purple Rain*

Run DMC – *Raising Hell*

L L Cool J – *Radio*

Stevie Wonder – *Talking Book*

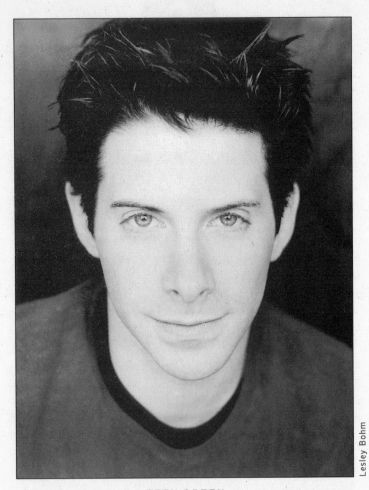

SETH GREEN

Lesley Bohm

SETH GREEN
Actor

Michael Jackson – *Thriller*

The Beatles – *The Beatles* ("White Album")

U2 – *Achtung Baby*

Jane's Addiction – *Ritual de lo Habitual*

Dr. Dre – *The Chronic*

The Beastie Boys – *Ill Communication*

Beck – *Odelay*

Remy Zero – *Villa Elaine*

Nirvana – *Nevermind*

Pink Floyd – *Wish You Were Here*

ROBIN TUNNEY
Actress

Grease – Original motion picture soundtrack

Bow Wow Wow – *I Want Candy*

Palace Songs – *Hope*

David Bowie – *The Rise and Fall of Ziggy Stardust and the Spiders from Mars*

The Beatles – *Anthology*

Tom Waits – *Anthology of Tom Waits*

Liz Phair – *Exile in Guyville*

Liz Phair – *White Chocolatespaceegg*

Mazzy Star – *So Tonight That I Might See*

Blur – *13*

JACKIE CHAN
Actor, martial artist

Sarah Brightman – *Eden*

Air Supply – *Lost in Love*

Lionel Richie – *Truly: The Love Song*

Wham! – *Make It Big*

Whitney Houston – *Whitney Houston*

David Tao – *David Tao*

Kitaro – *Silk Road*

Sarah Brightman – *The Andrew Lloyd Webber Collection*

Elvis Presley – *Blue Hawaii*

Beauty and the Beast – Original motion picture soundtrack (Mandarin version)

DAVID ARQUETTE
Actor

The Wailers – *Burnin'*

Chet Baker – *The Essential Chet Baker*

Al Green – *Greatest Hits*

Bill Withers – *Greatest Hits*

David Bowie – *The Rise and Fall of Ziggy Stardust and the Spiders from Mars*

Otis Redding – *Greatest Hits*

The Beatles – *The Beatles* ("White Album")

Pink Floyd – *Dark Side of the Moon*

The Jimi Hendrix Experience – *Smash Hits*

Radiohead – *The Bends*

JENNA ELFMAN
Actress

Hedwig and the Angry Inch –
Original cast recording

John Lee Hooker – *The Healer*

Tom Petty and the Heartbreakers – *Echo*

Garbage – *Version 2.0*

Etta James – *At Last!*

Janis Joplin – everything

Fleetwood Mac – *Rumours*

Prince and the Revolution – *Purple Rain*

Bob Dylan – *Planet Waves*

Beethoven – *Wellington's Victory*, op. 91

JASON PRIESTLEY
Actor, director

David Bowie – *Aladdin Sane*

Nirvana – *Unplugged*

Miles Davis – *Kind of Blue*

Frank Sinatra – *Songs for Young Lovers*

Chet Baker – *My Funny Valentine*

Elvis Costello and the Attractions –
This Year's Model

The Beatles – *Rubber Soul*

Dead Kennedys – *Plastic Surgery Disasters*

U2 – *The Joshua Tree*

Serge Gainsbourg – *Histoire de Melodie Nelson*

JASON PRIESTLEY

STEVEN SEAGAL
Actor, martial artist

Albert Collins – *Showdown*

Lightnin' Hopkins – *Lightnin' in New York* (live)

Howlin' Wolf – *Best of Howlin' Wolf*

Muddy Waters – *Hard Again*

John Lee Hooker – *Alternative Boogie: Early Studio Recordings: 1948–1952*

B.B. King – *Live at the Apollo*

Clarence "Gatemouth" Brown – *Alright Again!*

Plastic Slap – *This Modern Age 1*

Slim Harpo – *Baby, Scratch My Back*

The Jimi Hendrix Experience – *Are You Experienced?*

LAURA DERN
Actress

The Jimi Hendrix Experience –
Are You Experienced?

The Allman Brothers Band – *Live at
Fillmore East*

Ben Harper – *The Will to Live*

Stevie Wonder – *Talking Book*

John Prine – *Great Days: The John
Prine Anthology*

Little Feat – *Dixie Chicken*

Kate Bush – *The Kick Inside*

Elton John – *Goodbye Yellow Brick Road*

Led Zeppelin – *(IV)*

Fleetwood Mac – *Rumours*

HENRY WINKLER

HENRY WINKLER
Actor, director

Blood, Sweat & Tears with Al Kooper –
The Child Is Father to the Man

The Beach Boys – *Pet Sounds*

Jennifer Warnes – *Famous Blue Raincoat*

Elton John – *The One*

The Moody Blues – *In Search of the Lost Chord*

Pink Floyd – *The Wall*

Billy Joel – *Greatest Hits, Vols. I & II*

Johnny Mathis – *Johnny's Greatest Hits*

Nat King Cole – *Love Is the Thing*

Jennifer Warnes – *In the Wee Small Hours*

ED BURNS
Actor, director

Bruce Springsteen – *Darkness on the Edge of Town*

Bruce Springsteen – *Tunnel of Love*

Led Zeppelin – *I*

Led Zeppelin – *II*

Rolling Stones – *Some Girls*

Pete Yourn – *Music for the Morning After*

Pearl Jam – *Ten*

Guns N' Roses – *Appetite for Destruction*

Alice in Chains – *Jar of Flies*

BILLY ZANE
Actor

Nick Drake – *Pink Moon*

The Rolling Stones – *Exile on Main Street*

Muddy Waters – *Muddy & The Wolf*

The The – *Dusk*

The Cure – *Staring at the Sea: The Singles*

Stan Getz – *Jazz Samba*

Led Zeppelin – *Led Zeppelin*

Puccini – *Selected Arias*

The Velvet Underground – *VU*

David Bowie – *The Rise and Fall of
Ziggy Stardust and the Spiders from Mars*

ANDY DICK
Actor

Abba – *Gold*

All That Jazz – Original soundtrack

XTC – *Skylarking*

Rickie Lee Jones – *The Magazine*

Laurie Anderson – *Big Science/Strange Angels*

Hank Williams – *The Complete Hank Williams*
(boxed set)

Van Morrison – *Astral Weeks*

Ani DiFranco – *Dilate*

Orchestral Manoeuvres in the Dark –
The Pacific Age

Whale – *We Care*

ANDY DICK

WINONA RYDER
Actress

Bruce Springsteen – *Nebraska*

Tom Waits – *Closing Time*

Pearl Jam – *Ten*

U2 – *Boy*

Fairground Attraction – *The First of a
Million Kisses*

The Replacements – *Tim*

The Clash – *Combat Rock*

The Pretenders – *Pretenders*

Wilco – *A.M.*

Soul Asylum – *Hang Time*

Singers
and
Musicians

ROB ZOMBIE

ROB ZOMBIE
White Zombie

The Beatles – *The Beatles* ("White Album")

Alice Cooper – *Love It to Death*

Kiss – *Destroyer*

Black Sabbath – *Sabotage*

Ramones – *It's Alive*

Blondie – *Plastic Letters*

Frank Sinatra – *Songs for Swingin' Lovers!*

Tom Waits – *Rain Dogs*

Cheap Trick – *Live at Budokan*

Slim Whitman – *Greatest Hits*

GAVIN ROSSDALE
Bush

Siouxsie and the Banshees – *The Scream*

Public Image Ltd. – *Metal Box*

The Fall – *The Marshall Suite*

The Pixies – *Surfer Rosa*

Fugazi – *Red Medicine*

Slint – *Spiderland*

Shellac – *1000 Hurts*

Massive Attack – *Mezzanine*

Underworld – *Beacoup Fish*

The Jesus Lizard – *Goat*

JOHN TAYLOR
Duran Duran

The Beatles – *Meet the Beatles!*

Beethoven – *Immortal Beloved* soundtrack

David Bowie – *The Rise and Fall of
Ziggy Stardust and the Spiders from Mars*

Genesis – *Selling England by the Pound*

The Sex Pistols – *Never Mind the Bollocks
Here's the Sex Pistols*

Chic – *Risqué*

Mozart – *Amadeus* soundtrack
(conducted by Neville Marriner)

Miles Davis – *Kind of Blue*

Duke Ellington – *Jazz Party*

Nirvana – *Nevermind*

ALICE COOPER
Musician

The Yardbirds – *Having a Rave Up
with the Yardbirds*

The Rolling Stones – *England's
Newest Hitmakers*

The Doors – *Strange Days*

Paul Butterfield – *East-West*

West Side Story – Original cast recording

Burt Bacharach – *Reaching Out*

Laura Nyro – *Eli and the 13th Confession*

The Beatles – *The Beatles* ("White Album")

The Beach Boys – *Pet Sounds*

Love – *Da Capo*

ALICE COOPER

FLEA
Red Hot Chili Peppers

The Germs – *G.I.*

Funkadelic – *Hardcore Jollies*

Bob Marley and the Wailers – *Catch a Fire*

John Coltrane – *Blue Train*

Gang of Four – *Entertainment*

The Jimi Hendrix Experience –
Axis: Bold as Love

Miles Davis – *Kind of Blue*

Ice Cube – *AmeriKKKa's Most Wanted*

Neil Young – *Tonight's the Night*

Fugazi – *Red Medicine*

NIKKI SIXX
Mötley Crüe

David Bowie – *Diamond Dogs*

The Rolling Stones – *Black and Blue*

Kiss – *Hotter Than Hell*

Black Sabbath – *Sabbath Bloody Sabbath*

Aerosmith – *Get Your Wings*

Queen – *Queen II*

Mötley Crüe – *Too Fast for Love*

Iggy and the Stooges – *Raw Power*

Alice Cooper – *Killer*

58 – *Diet for a New America*

SAMMY HAGAR
Musician

Cream – *Fresh Cream*

The Beatles – *Abbey Road*

Procol Harum – *Procol Harum*

Led Zeppelin – *II*

Peter Gabriel – "Games Without Frontiers"
album (his third, untitled)

Pink Floyd – *Dark Side of the Moon*

The Who – *Who's Next*

The Rolling Stones – *Exile on Main Street*

Otis Redding – *The Immortal Otis Redding*

Van Morrison – *Moondance*

SHIRLEY MANSON
Garbage

Marianne Faithfull – *Broken English*

David Bowie – *The Rise and Fall of Ziggy Stardust and the Spiders from Mars*

Patti Smith – *Horses*

Television – *Marquee Moon*

The Pretenders – *Pretenders*

The Stone Roses – *The Stone Roses*

Radiohead – *The Bends*

Frank Sinatra – *The Capitol Years*

The Beatles – *The Beatles* ("White Album")

Siouxsie and the Banshees – *The Scream*

HANSON

Dewey Nicks

HANSON
Musicians

Fleetwood Mac – *Rumours*

Michael Jackson – *Thriller*

U2 – *The Joshua Tree*

The Rolling Stones – *Exile on Main Street*

Paul Simon – *Graceland*

Bob Dylan – *Blood on the Tracks*

Eagles – *Their Greatest Hits (1971–1975)*

Billy Joel – *Innocent Man*

The Beatles – *Rubber Soul*

The Jimi Hendrix Experience –
Electric Ladyland

RICK JAMES
Musician

Stevie Wonder – *Songs in the Key of Life*

Miles Davis – *Sketches of Spain*

Marvin Gaye – *Let's Get It On*

John Coltrane – *My Favorite Things*

Aretha Franklin – *Lady Soul*

Tina Marie – *Irons in the Fire*

The Beatles – *Sgt. Pepper's Lonely Hearts
Club Band*

Gato Barbieri – *Caliente*

Joni Mitchell – *Court and Spark*

Crosby, Stills, and Nash – *Crosby Stills & Nash*

RUFUS WAINWRIGHT
Musician

Maria Callas – *La Divina*

Nina Simone – *My Baby Just Cares for Me*

Serge Gainsbourg – *Comic Strip*

Rameau – *Castor et Pollux*
(William Christy and Les Arts Florrisants)

Elvis Presley – *The Sun Sessions*

Stravinsky – *The Firebird*

Verdi – *Otello* (with Placido Domingo
and Renata Scotto)

Peggy Lee – *Black Coffee*

Duke Ellington – *The Queen Suites*

Kate and Anna McGarrigle – *Dancer with
Bruised Knees*

KOOL KEITH
Musician

Ultramagnetic MC's – *Critical Beatdown*

Eric B. & Rakim – *Paid in Full*

Public Enemy – *Yo! Bum Rush the Show*

Mo B. Dick – *Gangsta Harmony*

Mia X – *Mama Drama*

Kool Keith – *Black Elvis*

Dr. Dooom – *First Come, First Served*

H-Town – *Begging After Dark*

E-40 – *In a Major Way*

Prodigy – *The Fat of the Land*

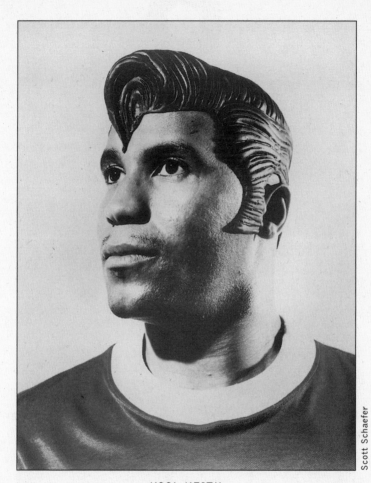

KOOL KEITH

Scott Schaefer

HENRY ROLLINS
Musician, author, actor

John Coltrane – *A Love Supreme*

The Beatles – *Abbey Road*

The Velvet Underground – *The Velvet Underground and Nico* (first album)

The Stooges – *Funhouse*

Thin Lizzy – *Jailbreak*

Ruts – *The Crack*

Rites of Spring – *End on End*

The Jimi Hendrix Experience – *Electric Ladyland*

James Brown – *Revolution of the Mind*

Bob Dylan – *Blonde on Blonde*

www.21361.com

RAY MANZEREK
The Doors

John Coltrane – *Olé Coltrane*

Stravinsky – *Stravinsky Conducts
"The Rite of Spring"*

Muddy Waters – *Best of Muddy Waters*

Miles Davis and Gil Evans – *Sketches of Spain*

Ravi Shankar – *Improvisations:
Theme from "Pather Panchali"*

Copland – *Billy the Kid*; *Rodeo*
(conducted by Leonard Bernstein)

Howlin' Wolf – *Moanin' in the Moonlight*

The Jimi Hendrix Experience – *Axis: Bold as Love*

The Beatles – *Rubber Soul*

X – *Los Angeles*

JEFF BECK
Musician

The Beach Boys – *Pet Sounds*

Billy Cobham – *Spectrum*

Stevie Wonder – *Music of My Mind*

William Orbit – *Strange Cargo 1, 2 & 3*

Gene Vincent & His Blue Caps – "Lotta Lovin'"

Prince – *Sign o' the Times*

Sly and the Family Stone – *There's a Riot Goin' On*

ROB THOMAS
Matchbox 20

Stevie Wonder – *Songs in the Key of Life*

Indigo Girls – *Indigo Girls*

Paul Simon – *Graceland*

Willie Nelson – *Greatest Hits*
(& Some That Will Be)

Peter Gabriel – *Us*

Michael Jackson – *Off the Wall*

The Beatles – *The Beatles* ("White Album")

Tom Petty – *Full Moon Fever*

Pink Floyd – *The Wall*

Elton John – *Goodbye Yellow Brick Road*

BRIAN MCKNIGHT
Musician

Michael Jackson – *Off the Wall*

Stevie Wonder – *Hotter Than July*

Donald Fagen – *The Nightfly*

Michael Jackson – *Thriller*

Steely Dan – *Gaucho*

Lionel Richie – *Can't Slow Down*

DeBarge – *Rhythm of the Night*

A Tribe Called Quest – *Midnight Marauders*

Nat King Cole Trio – *Live at the Savoy*

The Notorious B.I.G. – *Ready to Die*

BRIAN MCKNIGHT

Kwaku Alston

DAVID BOWIE
Musician

Brian Eno – *Music for Airports*

Little Richard – *She's Got It*

Lou Reed – *Transformer*

T-Rex – *Cosmic Dance*

Johnny Cash – *The Man in Black*

The Pixies – *Doolittle*

Grace Jones – *Nightclubbing*

Prince – *1999*

Psychedelic Furs – *Forever Now*

Prodigy – *Music for the Jilted Generation*

NICK HEXUM
311

The Clash – *London Calling*

Bob Marley & the Wailers – *Natty Dread*

Bad Brains – *Quickness*

The Smiths – *Louder Than Bombs*

De La Soul – *Buhloone Mindstate*

U2 – *Achtung Baby*

The Beastie Boys – *Check Your Head*

Led Zeppelin – *Houses of the Holy*

XTC – *Skylarking*

Jane's Addiction – *Nothing's Shocking*

GENE SIMMONS
Kiss

The Jimi Hendrix Experience – *Are You Experienced?*

Spencer Davis Group – *Autumn*

The Rolling Stones – *Between the Buttons*

The Everly Brothers – *Greatest Hits*

Dave Clark Five – *Hits*

The Temptations – *Hits*

Ray Charles – *Georgia*

Chubby Checker – *Let's Twist Again*

The Who – *Tommy*

The Beatles – *The Beatles* ("White Album")

GENE SIMMONS

J. MASCIS
Dinosaur Jr.

Eater – *Complete Eater*

The Rolling Stones – *Exile on Main Street*

Sandy Denny – *The Best of Sandy Denny*

Blind Faith – *Blind Faith*

The Stooges – *Fun House*

Wipers – *Over the Edge*

Black Sabbath – *Sabotage*

Wire – *Pink Flag*

13th Floor Elevators – *Easter Everywhere*

Ron Wood – *I've Got My Own Album to Do*

MEATLOAF
Musician

The Beatles – *Sgt. Pepper's Lonely Hearts Club Band*

Queen – *News of the World*

The Kingston Trio – *From the Hungry I*

The Eagles – *Hotel California*

Bob Seger – *Against the Wind*

Rodgers and Hammerstein – *Oklahoma!*

Doug Clark & Hot Nuts – *Doug Clark & Hot Nuts, Vol. 1*

Ella Fitzgerald and Louis Armstrong – *Porgy and Bess*

Stevie Wonder – *Innervisions*

Bob Dylan – *Highway 61 Revisited*

TRICKY
Musician

Kate Bush – *The Whole Story*

Noreaga – *N.O.R.E.*

Wu Tang Clan – *Enter the Wu-Tang
(36 Chambers)*

Paul Weller – *Paul Weller*

Public Enemy – *It Takes a Nation of Millions
to Hold Us Back*

Rakim – *The 18th Letter*

Slick Rick – *The Art of Storytelling*

The Specials – *Specials Are Go*

Fun Boy Three – *Fame*

N.W.A. – *Straight Outta Compton*

STEVE VAI
Musician

Queen – *Queen II*

West Side Story – Original Broadway
cast recording

Frank Zappa – *Jazz from Hell*

David Bowie – *The Rise and Fall of
Ziggy Stardust and the Spiders from Mars*

Jeff Buckley – *Grace*

Led Zeppelin – *II*

Prince – *Sign o' the Times*

Alice Cooper – *Billion Dollar Babies*

Elton John – *Goodbye Yellow Brick Road*

Jethro Tull – *A Passion Play*

SARAH MCLACHLAN

SARAH MCLACHLAN
Musician

Talk Talk – *Spirit of Eden*

Peter Gabriel – *Passion*

Tom Waits – *Closing Time*

Joni Mitchell – *Blue*

Brian Eno – *Thursday Afternoon*

Willie Nelson – *Stardust*

Fleetwood Mac – *Rumours*

Peter Gabriel – *So*

Sinead O'Connor – *Universal Mother*

Annie Lennox – *Diva*

STEVEN PAGE
Barenaked Ladies

Harry Nilsson – *Nilsson Sings Newman*

The Lilac Time – *Paradise Circus*

Leonard Cohen – *Death of a Ladies' Man*

Rheostatics – *Whale Music*

American Music Club – *Mercury*

Elvis Costello and the Attractions –
Blood & Chocolate

Prefab Sprout – *Steve McQueen*

The Beatles – *The Beatles* ("White Album")

Tom Waits – *Swordfishtrombones*

The Smiths – *Hatful of Hollow*

MOBY
Musician

Roxy Music – *Roxy Music*

The Rolling Stones – *Goat's Head Soup*

The Beatles – *The Beatles* ("White Album")

Kraftwerk – *The Man Machine*

Prince and the Revolution – *Purple Rain*

Massive Attack – *Protection*

Creedence Clearwater Revival – *Chronicle, Vol. 1*

Nick Drake – *Bryter Layter*

Public Enemy – *It Takes a Nation of Millions to Hold Us Back*

Joy Division – *Closer*

Television – *Marquee Moon*

SLASH
Guns N' Roses; Slash's Snakepit

The Rolling Stones – *Let It Bleed*

Stevie Wonder – *Songs in the Key of Life*

Jeff Beck – *Blow by Blow*

Aerosmith – *Rocks*

Led Zeppelin – *II*

The Rolling Stones – *Exile on Main Street*

Joni Mitchell – *Miles of Aisles*

Cat Stevens – *Tea for the Tillerman*

AC/DC – *Highway to Hell*

Mellow Moods compilation

Antony Medley

SLASH

DAVID GROHL
Nirvana; Foo Fighters

Bad Brains – *Rock for Light*

The Pixies – *Trompe le Monde*

The Melvins – *Gluey Porch Treatments*

Kyuss – *Blues for the Red Sun*

Led Zeppelin – *Coda*

Voivod – *Rrröööaaarrr*

Hüsker Dü – *Zen Arcade*

Black Sabbath – all

Slayer – *Reign in Blood*

The Beatles – *Rubber Soul*

THE BEE GEES
Musicians

The Beach Boys – *Pet Sounds*

The Beatles – *Sgt. Pepper's Lonely Hearts Club Band*

Elvis Presley – "Heartbreak Hotel" and "Jailhouse Rock"

Frank Sinatra – all

Michael Jackson – *Thriller*

The Jimi Hendrix Experience – *Are You Experienced?*

The Band – *Music from Big Pink*

Everly Brothers – *Greatest Hits*

Patsy Cline – *The Essential Patsy Cline*

Rod Stewart – *Every Picture Tells a Story*

Autumn deWilde

ELLIOTT SMITH

ELLIOTT SMITH
Musician

The Beatles – *The Beatles* ("White Album")

The Saints – *Eternally Yours*

Quasi – *Featuring "Birds"*

The Rolling Stones – *Exile on Main Street*

The Beatles – *Magical Mystery Tour*

My Bloody Valentine – *Loveless*

Bob Dylan – *Blood on the Tracks*

Pavement – *Crooked Rain, Crooked Rain*

Stevie Wonder – *Songs in the Key of Life*

Television – *Marquee Moon*

JAMES IHA
Smashing Pumpkins

My Bloody Valentine – *Isn't Anything*

The Stooges – *Funhouse*

Whiskeytown – *Strangers Almanac*

Tom Waits – *The Asylum Years*

Frank Sinatra – *The Capitol Years*

Syd Barrett – *The Madcap Laughs*

Sly and the Family Stone – *Anthology*

The Beatles – *The Beatles* ("White Album")

The Clash – *London Calling*

Ennio Morricone – *Cinema Paradiso*
original motion picture soundtrack

RICHARD PATRICK
Filter

Jane's Addiction – *Nothing's Shocking*

Soundgarden – *Superunknown*

Led Zepellin – *Physical Graffiti*

Ministry – *The Land of Rape and Honey*

Chris Isaak – *Wicked Ways: Anthology*

The Doors – *The Doors*

Skinny Puppy – *VIVISect VI*

Patsy Cline – *12 Greatest Hits*

The Beatles – *Sgt. Pepper's Lonely Hearts Club Band*

Neil Diamond – *Hot August Night*

JOHN TESH

JOHN TESH
Musician

Peter Gabriel – *So*

The Beatles – *The Beatles* ("White Album")

Jethro Tull – *Thick as a Brick*

The Beatles – *Sgt. Pepper's Lonely Hearts
Club Band*

The Jimi Hendrix Experience –
Are You Experienced?

Yes – *Close to the Edge*

Steely Dan – *Aja*

Pink Floyd – *The Wall*

The Doors – *Morrison Hotel*

Led Zeppelin – *(IV)*

LOU REED
Musician

Ornette Coleman – *Change of the Century*

Al Green – *Belle Album*

Scott Walker – *Tilt*

Bob Dylan – *Blood on the Tracks*

Little Richard – The Specialty boxed set

Hank Williams – *Original Singles
Collection . . . Plus*

The Anthology of American Folk Music
(compiled by Harry Smith)

Rahsaan Roland Kirk – *Does Your House Have
Lions: The Rahsaan Roland Kirk Anthology*

Lorraine Ellison – *Stay with Me*

Laurie Anderson – "O Superman
(for Massanet)" on *Big Science*

MELISSA AUF DER MAUR
Hole; Smashing Pumpkins

Kyuss – *Blues for the Red Sun*

The Beach Boys – *Pet Sounds*

Smashing Pumpkins – *Gish*

Soul Side – *Soon Came Happy*

Failure – *Comfort*

Girls Against Boys – *Venus Luxure No. 1 Baby*

The Velvet Underground –
The Velvet Underground and Nico
(with Warhol banana)

The Smiths – *Hatful of Hollow*

Blondie – *Parallel Lines*

Tinker – *Receiver*

TIONNE "T-BOZ" WATKINS
TLC

Michael Jackson – *Thriller*

Prince – *The Hits 1, 2, and 3*

NWA – *Niggaz4life*

Eazy-E – *Eazy Duz It*

2Pac – *All Eyez on Me*

The Cranberries – *No Need to Argue*

Paula Cole – *This Fire*

Mary J. Blige – *What's the 411?*

Juvenile – *400 Degreez*

Michael Jackson – *Off the Wall*

TIONNE "T-BOZ" WATKINS

THOMAS DOLBY
Musician

Van Morrison – *Astral Weeks*

Joni Mitchell – *Hejira*

David Bowie – *Low*

Iggy Pop – *The Idiot*

Kraftwerk – *Trans-Europe Express*

Talking Heads – *Remain in Light*

Prince – *Sign o' the Times*

The Beatles – *Magical Mystery Tour*

The Beach Boys – *Surf's Up*

Frank Zappa – *Apostrophe*

MARK HOPPUS
Blink-182

Jimmy Eat World – *Clarity*

Get Up Kids – *Something to Write Home About*

Jimmy Eat World – *Static Prevails*

The Promise Ring – *Nothing Feels Good*

Far – *Water & Solutions*

NOFX – *Punk in Drublic*

Bad Religion – *No Control*

Lemonheads – *It's a Shame About Ray*

Ned's Atomic Dustbin – *God Fodder*

Face to Face – *Don't Turn Away*

"WEIRD AL" YANKOVIC
Musician

Spike Jones – *The Best of Spike Jones, Vol. 1*

Stan Freberg – *The Best of Stan Freberg*

Allan Sherman – *My Son, the Folk Singer*

Tom Lehrer – *That Was the Year That Was* (live)

Shel Silverstein – *Freakin' at the Freakers' Ball*

The Credibility Gap – *A Great Gift Idea*

Devo – *Are We Not Men?*

The B-52's – *The B-52's*

The Kinks – *The Kinks Present A Soap Opera*

The Mothers of Invention – *Absolutely Free*

Johnny Buzzerio

"WEIRD AL" YANKOVIC

MARK MCGRATH
Sugar Ray

The Beach Boys – *Pet Sounds*

The Cult – *Love*

Guns N' Roses – *Appetite for Destruction*

Weezer – *Weezer*

Mobb Deep – *The Infamous*

The Beastie Boys – *License to Ill*

Willie Nelson – *Always on My Mind*

Slayer – *Reign in Blood*

Supercat – *Don Dada*

Gregory Isaacs – *Night Nurse*

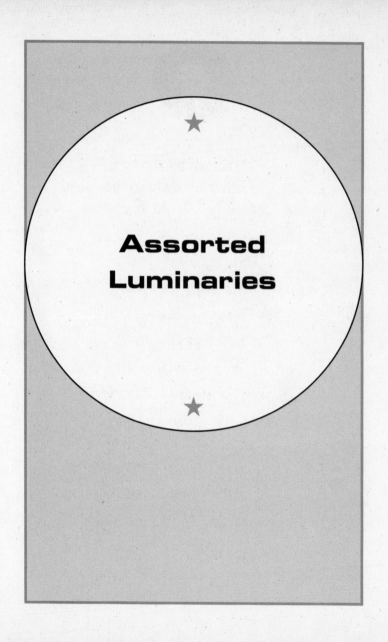

Assorted
Luminaries

TODD ZEILE
Professional baseball player,
New York Mets

Led Zeppelin – *(IV)*

Pink Floyd – *The Wall*

The Beatles – *Abbey Road*

Michael Jackson – *Thriller*

Elton John – *Greatest Hits*

Queen – *News of the World*

Metallica – *Live with the
San Francisco Symphony*

Red Hot Chili Peppers – *Californication*

Creed – *Human Clay*

Saturday Night Fever soundtrack

Wayne Williams

TODD ZEILE

RON JEREMY
Porn star

Chopin – Piano concertos

Handel and Bach

Jethro Tull – *Aqualung*

Traffic – *The Low Spark of High Heeled Boys*

Guns N' Roses – *Use Your Illusion I & II*

Kid Rock – *Devil Without a Cause*

Michael Flatley – *Lord of the Dance*
musical score

Dave Koz, saxophonist

Celine Dion – *The Best of Celine Dion*

Digital Underground – "Humpty Dance"
on *Sex Packets*

MONICA LEWINSKY
Former White House intern, designer

Rodgers and Hammerstein – *Cinderella*
television soundtrack

Dave Matthews Band – *Live at Luther College*

Violent Femmes – "Blister in the Sun"

Ella Fitzgerald – *The First Lady of Jazz*

Guys and Dolls soundtrack

Sarah McLachlan – *Surfacing*

Frank Sinatra – *Songs for Swingin' Lovers!*

Ben Harper – "Sexual Healing" on
Please Bleed (CD-single)

The Flying Neutrinos – *Hotel Child*

Depeche Mode – *Catching Up with
Depeche Mode*

DAVID COPPERFIELD

Michael Thompson

DAVID COPPERFIELD
Magician

The Rolling Stones – *Exile on Main Street*

The Clash – *London Calling*

Bruce Springsteen – *Greetings from Asbury Park*

The Beatles – *The Beatles* ("White Album")

Stevie Wonder – *Songs in the Key of Life*

Moby – *Play*

Nirvana – *Nevermind*

Peter Gabriel – *So*

The Jimi Hendrix Experience – *Are You Experienced?*

Bob Dylan – *Bringing It All Back Home*

SALLY JESSE RAPHAEL
Talk-show host

Edith Piaf – *The Voice of the Sparrow:
The Very Best of Edith Piaf*

Tchaikovsky – *The Nutcracker Suite*

Charles Aznavour – *Aznavour Live:
Palais des Congrès*

Kismet – Original Broadway cast recording

Chicago – *Greatest Hits*

Mame – Original Broadway cast recording

Hooked on Classics compilation

Chop Wood, Carry Water compilation

Billy Idol – "White Wedding"

Peter Mayle – *A Year in Provence*

HOWIE MANDEL
Comedian

Pink Floyd – *Dark Side of the Moon*
Steve Martin – *Let's Get Small*

Note: "These are the only two albums I bought."

FABIO
Model

Journey – *Greatest Hits*

Simple Minds – *Live in the City of Light*

Van Halen – *For Unlawful Carnal Knowledge*

Paul Hardcastle – *The Jazzmasters* series

Greg Chaquico – *Acoustic Highway*

The Beatles – *Sgt. Pepper's Lonely Hearts Club Band*

Kristine W. – *Land of the Living*

Lenny Kravitz – *5*

Jamiroquai – "Cosmic Girl" on *Travelling Without Moving*

Stevie Wonder – *Songs in the Key of Life*

FABIO

NANCY O'DELL
Co-anchor of *Access Hollywood*

The Beatles – *The Beatles* ("White Album")

Michael Jackson – *Thriller*

Eagles – *Hotel California*

Fleetwood Mac – *Rumours*

Carole King – *Tapestry*

The Beatles – *Sgt. Pepper's Lonely Hearts Club Band*

The Beach Boys – *Pet Sounds*

Prince and the Revolution – *Purple Rain*

U2 – *The Joshua Tree*

Pink Floyd – *The Wall*

TREY PARKER
South Park co-creator

Elton John – *Captain Fantastic and the Brown Dirt Cowboy*

AC/DC – *Back in Black*

Van Halen – *Diver Down*

Prince and the Revolution – *Purple Rain*

The Cure – *Disintegration*

Primus – *Sailing the Seas of Cheese*

Mel Tormé and George Shearing – *A Vintage Year*

G. Love & Special Sauce – *Philadelphonic*

Carl Orff – *Carmina Burana*

Mel Tormé – *The Mel Tormé Collection* (4-CD boxed set)

H. Kluetmeier

SCOTT HAMILTON

SCOTT HAMILTON
Figure skater

Roxy Music – *Avalon*

Pink Floyd – *Dark Side of the Moon*

Led Zeppelin – *Physical Graffiti*

Eagles – *Hotel California*

Bruce Springsteen – *Born to Run*

The Who – *Who's Next*

Cheap Trick – *Live at Budokan*

Joe Walsh – *Look What I Did*

Steely Dan – *Aja*

The Beatles – *The Beatles* ("White Album")

DR. DREW PINSKY
Co-host of *Loveline*

The Doobie Brothers – *Minute by Minute*

The Rolling Stones – *Through the Past, Darkly
(Big Hits, Vol. 2)*

The Doors – *The Doors*

Donizetti – *Lucia di Lammermour* (with Luciano
Pavorati, Sherrill Milnes, and Joan Sutherland)

Die Fledermaus Gala (conducted by
Herbert Von Karajan)

Richard Pryor – *Supernigger*

Led Zepellin – *Led Zeppelin*

Louis Armstrong – *Great Chicago Concert 1956*

Concert for Bangladesh (with George Harrison,
Ringo Star, Leon Russell)

Joe Cocker – *Mad Dogs & Englishmen*

TARA LIPINSKI
Figure skater

Michael Jackson – *Thriller*

The Bodyguard soundtrack

Madonna – *Ray of Light*

Nirvana – *Nevermind*

Saturday Night Fever soundtrack

George Michael – *Faith*

Mariah Carey – *Butterfly*

Destiny's Child – *The Writing's on the Wall*

Fleetwood Mac – *Rumours*

Blondie – *The Best of Blondie*

JACKIE COLLINS
Author

Marvin Gaye – *What's Going On*

El De Barge – *Heart Mind & Soul*

Sade – *Diamond Life*

Astrud Gilberto – *The Warm World of Astrud Gilberto*

Michael Jackson – *Thriller*

Harold Melvin and the Blue Notes – "Don't Leave Me This Way"

Frank Sinatra – *In the Wee Small Hours*

Saturday Night Fever soundtrack

Stevie Wonder – *Songs in the Key of Life*

Francis Albert Sinatra and Antonio Carlos Jobim

JACKIE COLLINS

PAMELA DES BARRES
Author, rock groupie

The Jimi Hendrix Experience –
Are You Experienced?

Terence Trent D'Arby – *Introducing the Hardline
According to Terence Trent D'Arby*

Chet Baker – *Chet Baker Sings*

Dwight Yoakam – *Buenos Noches from
a Lonely Room*

The Flying Burrito Brothers –
The Gilded Palace of Sin

Elvis Presley – *Jailhouse Rock*

Bob Dylan – *Bringing It All Back Home*

The Beatles – *Meet the Beatles!*

The Rolling Stones – *Beggars Banquet*

Sam Cooke – *The Man Who Invented Soul*

ANKA RADAKOVICH
Author, *Playboy*, *Maxim* sex columnist

Sex Pistols – *Never Mind the Bollocks
Here's the Sex Pistols*

Hole – *Live Through This*

The Slits – "Girls Bite Back" (single)

The Muffs – *Hamburger*

Butthole Surfers – *The Hole Truth . . .
and Nothing Butt*

Pussy Galore – "Penetration in the Centerfold"
on *Sugarshit Sharp*

Circle Jerks – *Group Sex*

The Vibrators – *We Vibrate:
The Best of the Vibrators*

The Humpers – *Plastique Valentine*

Hard Ons – *Dick Cheese*

TONY HAWK
Pro skateboarder

The Beatles – *Sgt. Pepper's Lonely Hearts
Club Band*

The Clash – *London Calling*

Best of Rodney on the Roq compilation

De La Soul – *De La Soul Is Dead*

Peter Gabriel – *Passion*

Danny Elfman – *Dead Presidents* soundtrack

Kraftwerk – *Electric Café*

Jane's Addiction – *Nothing's Shocking*

Nine Inch Nails – *The Fragile*

Madonna – *The Immaculate Collection*

TONY HAWK

ADAM CAROLLA
Co-host of *The Man Show*
and *Loveline*

Joe Jackson – *Look Sharp!*

John Hiatt – *All of a Sudden*

John Hiatt – *Bring the Family*

John Hiatt – *Walk On*

Graham Parker – *The Up Escalator*

Led Zeppelin – *Physical Graffiti*

The Spinners – *The Best of the Spinners*

Elvis Costello and the Attractions –
Armed Forces

UFO – *Live*

Boston – *Boston*

PENN JILLETTE
Comedian, magician

The Velvet Underground – *The Velvet Underground and Nico*

Bob Dylan – *Blonde on Blonde*

Lou Reed – *Street Hassle*

Flanders and Swann – *At the Drop of a Hat*

Stravinsky – *Rite of Spring*

John Lennon – *John Lennon and the Plastic Ono Band*

The Residents – *The Commercial Album*

Jonathan Richman and the Modern Lovers

Kramer – *Secret of Comedy*

David Allan Coe – *Underground*

Various artists – *The Song Poets*

KATO KAELIN

KATO KAELIN
Actor, O.J. Simpson houseguest

Radiohead – *Pablo Honey*

The Beatles – *Revolver*

The Beatles – *Rubber Soul*

George Harrison – *All Things Must Pass*

T-Rex – *The Slider*

Bruce Springsteen – *Greetings from
Asbury Park*

Queen – *Queen*

Billy Joel – *Piano Man*

The Alarm – *Standards*

Harry Shearer – *O.J. on Trial: The Early Years*

DENNIS RODMAN
Professional basketball player

Live – *Mental Jewelry*

Pearl Jam – *Ten*

The Jimi Hendrix Experience –
Are You Experienced?

Janis Joplin – *Greatest Hits*

Slade – *Feel the Noize: Greatest Hits*

Red Hot Chili Peppers – *Mother's Milk*

The Doors – *Greatest Hits*

Van Halen – *1984*

Stone Temple Pilots – *Purple*

Sublime – *Sublime*

MATT STONE
South Park co-creator

AC/DC – *Back in Black*

Rush – *Exit Stage Left*

John Coltrane – *A Love Supreme*

Stevie Wonder – *Songs in the Key of Life*

The Police – *Ghost in the Machine*

Radiohead – *OK Computer*

Primus – *Frizzle Fry*

Bow Wow Wow – *See Jungle! See Jungle!*

Talking Heads – *Fear of Music*

Funkadelic – *Maggot Brain*

SHAQUILLE O'NEAL

SHAQUILLE O'NEAL
Professional basketball player,
L.A. Lakers

Parliament – *Get the Funk Up*

Commodores – *Commodores*

Lakeside – *Fantastic Voyage*

Prince – *1999*

Earth, Wind and Fire – *Gratitude*

Queen – *The Game*

Sade – *Stronger Than Pride*

Run DMC – *Raising Hell*

Aerosmith – *Toys in the Attic*

Michael Jackson – *Thriller*

JOAN RIVERS
Comedienne

Frank Sinatra – anything

Al Green – *Greatest Hits*

Shania Twain – *Come on Over*

Macy Gray – *On How Life Is*

Mary Wells – *The Best of Mary Wells*

The Beatles – *The Beatles* ("White Album")

Patti Labelle – *Live at the Apollo*

Any original Broadway cast album

The Graduate soundtrack

Respect—A Century of Women in Music

Eminem – *The Marshall Mathers LP*

TYRESE
Model, actor, musician

Michael Jackson – *Off the Wall*

Destiny's Child – *The Writing's on the Wall*

Mary J. Blige – *My Life*

Luther Vandross – *The Best of Luther Vandross:*
The Best of Love

Brandy – *Never Say Never*

En Vogue – *Born to Sing*

Tyrese – *Tyrese*

R. Kelly – *R*

Janet Jackson – *Rhythm Nation 1814*

Baby Face – *Closer Look*

RUPAUL
Entertainer

Kenny Rogers – *Eyes That See in the Dark*

Dionne Warwick – *Heartbreaker*

Liza Minelli – *Results*

Diana Ross – *The Boss*

Michael Jackson – *Off the Wall*

Cher – *It's a Man's World*

Barbra Streisand – *Guilty*

Kool & the Gang – *All-time Greatest Hits*

Anita O'Day – *In a Mellow Tone*

Donna Summer – *Bad Girls*

Mathu Andersen

RUPAUL

VERONICA WEBB
Model, actress

Mozart Symphony no. 6

Outkast – *Atliens*

David Bowie – *Young Americans*

Public Enemy – *It Takes a Nation of Millions to Hold Us Back*

Clifford Brown – *Clifford Brown with Strings*

Notorious B.I.G. – *Life After Death*

Prince – *Sign o' the Times*

Miles Davis and Gil Evans – *Sketches of Spain*

Mahalia Jackson – *In the Upper Room*

Ravi Shankar – *Chants of India*

TODD OLDHAM
Fashion designer

Joni Mitchell – *Hejira*

Nirvana – *Unplugged*

Prince – *Sign o' the Times*

P. M. Dawn – *Jesus Wept*

Stevie Wonder – *Songs in the Key of Life*

Kruder & Dorfmeister – *G-Stoned* (EP)

The Clash – *Combat Rock*

Prince – *Lovesexy*

The Dave Brubeck Quartet – "Take Five"
(by Paul Desmond) on *Time Out*

Beck – *Midnite Vultures*

JIMMY VASSER

JIMMY VASSER
Race car driver

Led Zeppelin – any

The Police – *Outlandos D'Amour*

Frank Sinatra – *The Capitol Years*

The Sex Pistols – *Never Mind the Bollocks
Here's the Sex Pistols*

Bob Marley – *Natural Mystic*

Sublime – *Sublime*

Joni Mitchell – *Hits*

Bachelor Pad Royale (Ultra Lounge, Vol. 4)

Temple of the Dog – *Temple of the Dog*

Dr. Dre – *The Chronic*

MATT PINFIELD
Former MTV veejay, host of *Farmclub*

The Who – *Quadrophenia*

David Bowie – *The Rise and Fall of Ziggy Stardust and the Spiders from Mars*

The Beatles – *Revolver*

Buzzcocks – *A Different Kind of Tension*

The Rolling Stones – *Through the Past, Darkly (Big Hits, Vol. 2)*

Alice in Chains – *Dirt*

Soundgarden – *Superunknown*

The Clash – *London Calling*

The Jam – *All Mod Cons*

Oasis – *(What's the Story) Morning Glory?*

Acknowledgments

Kaysa and Alfred Friedman, Bucky McKay, Frida Aradottir, Peter Raspler, Adam Raspler, Orian Williams, David Diamond, Melissa Auf der Maur, David Dunton, Amanda Patten, Pierre Tremblay, Todd Fraser, Troy Agusto, Ian Noble, Daniella Cracknell, Brian Ling, Sarah Hada, Dorothy Hersey, Kate Morgan Biscoe, Kathy Keegan, Mike Watt, Amanda Lawrence, Laurel Sterns, Alison Leslie, Beth Franco, Dara Zweig, Brenda Feldman, Julia Heslin, Eric Kahn, Kal Weber, Steve Durand, Evsta Scholnick, Chip Butterman, Jono Hart, Chris Fenn, Alfred Hopton, Kathleen Kelly, Wendy Border, Erin Simonich, Monique Van Remortel, Jenni Weinman, Sherry Marsh, Alex Rozanski, Freda Friedman, and Winona Ryder (for being the first one in the book).

Special thanks to the music-loving celebrities who took part in the book and of course to the musicians who have inspired us all.

Index

Manson, Shirley, 47
Manzarek, Ray, 55
Mascius, J., 64
McGrath, Mark, 92
McKight, Brian, 58
McLachlan, Sarah, 69
Meatloaf, 65
Moby, 71
Moore, Thurston, 76
Morrow, Joshua, 16
O'Dell, Nancy, 104
Oldham, Todd, 129
O'Neal, Shaquille, 123
Page, Steven, 70
Parker, Trey, 105
Patrick, Richard, 81
Pinfield, Matt, 132
Pinsky, Dr. Drew, 108
Priestley, Jason, 26
Radakovich, Anka, 113
Raphael, Sally Jesse, 100
Reed, Lou, 84
Reubens, Paul, 3
Rivers, Joan, 124
Rodman, Dennis, 120
Rollins, Henry, 54
Rossdale, Gavin, 40
RuPaul, 126
Ryder, Winona, 36

Schwimmer, David, 19
Seagal, Steven, 28
Sevigny, Chloë, 14
Simmons, Gene, 62
Sixx, Nikki, 45
Slash, 72
Smith, Elliott, 79
Stone, Matt, 121
Taylor, John, 41
Tesh, John, 83
Thicke, Alan, 11
Thomas, Henry, 2
Thomas, Rob, 57
Thornton, Billy Bob, 15
Tricky, 66
Tunney, Robin, 22
Tyrese, 125
Vai, Steve, 67
Vasser, Jimmy, 131
Wainwright, Rufus, 51
Watkins, Tionne "T-Boz,"
   86
Watt, Mike, 75
Webb, Veronica, 128
Winkler, Henry, 31
Yankovic, "Weird Al," 90
Zane, Billy, 33
Zeile, Todd, 94
Zombie, Rob, 39